T0131490

# WHIP 5

## Journey Across the Galaxy

# TYLER JOHNS

authorHOUSE®

*AuthorHouse™*
*1663 Liberty Drive*
*Bloomington, IN 47403*
*www.authorhouse.com*
*Phone: 1 (800) 839-8640*

*Published by AuthorHouse   04/15/2020*

*ISBN: 978-1-7283-5883-3 (sc)*
*ISBN: 978-1-7283-5882-6 (e)*

# CONTENTS

# PROLOGUE

## The Epic Story of Whip Psy

Whip Psy is a psyvark (meaning "mind pig"). His friends are a crocodile named, Bobert "Bobi" Gatorson, and a black python named, Pition Vipers. Their adventures all started after their junior year in high school. Whip and his family went to East Virginia for their summer vacation to meet their longtime friends, the Andor family (anteaters), and to visit Whip's father, Tehran's brother, Seth. Tehran's father Ebenezer foretold that strange foreigners called the Vips, were about to rob their home city, and it was true. As the Psy family went home, Whip, Bobi, and Pition found out about the accident in a street junction by the shopping mall. The Vips' animals escaped. The three heroes fought the Vips and were granted a reward of $60,000. They all became rich. Whip built a traveling machine called the World Bug 3000. Whip found true love, the Vip king, Brendor's daughter, Zelda. She was held in prison and she mysteriously vanished.

On Christmas vacation, Tehran was confronted by a Russian white tiger royal family called the Satvrinskis. The mother was Tsarina Abmora and her son was Prince Aborabor. These tigers planned to make Whip's kid sister, Sarah, smart.

The Psy family along with Bobi and Pition drove to Canada, when suddenly, they met a walrus named, Fentruck Tusker, who was hired to find Tsarina Abmora. Whip, Bobi, and Pition visited the Satvrinskis' palace by teleporting through a portal from Canada to Russia. The three guys visited the Tsarina. Then on their way out, they stole two potions. Bobi and Pition drank a mythology potion, which allowed them to transform. Whip drank a potion of eternal life. After that, the heroes tried to rejoin the Psy family, but the Satvrinskis had them arrested.

Fortunately, the animals who escaped from the Vips came to Russia and helped the heroes escape. They adopted a giant squid to terrorize the town. They broke into the palace to save Sarah from the sacrifice of wisdom. But the sacrifice was made, and then Sarah accepted the wisdom but defied the Satvrinskis. She rejoined her family and Abmora turned angry. Fentruck Tusker came by to save the day and the heroes defeated Abmora.

After months after graduating from high school, Whip, Bobi, and Pition, along with Fentruck living with them, were going off to college. They drove to the Appalachian University in Harrisonburg, Virginia. They met all kinds of people there, like gangsters with rules and people and animals good at singing. Meanwhile, Tehran was at work in an office, but he got fired, so he had to join his son at college.

Whip and his pals participated in the College Amusers. They had rivals called the Arctics, who were a band of big cheaters. Tehran joined the Arctics to participate with them in the Amusers. The father and son competed against each other and the Arctics won by secretly cheating with gimmicks.

Later, Whip had a hard time with his father. Whip felt that the campus didn't fit for them both. Tehran had things to do. He had to get his grades up and to get off the Arctics' team.

And so, the big events of the College Amusers were on. Whip's team and the Arctics participated in a triathlon and Fentruck was somehow blasted ahead. The players had trouble and were about to be disqualified, so Whip summoned his father to join his team. As the triathlon went on, some teammates were put out for some occasional reasons and Whip had to race the Arctics' team leader, Angus Wellington, Jr., to the finish line. Whip won the whole tournament.

After three years of college, Whip, Bobi, Pition, and Fentruck heard about news on planet Mars. They flew in the World Bug 3000 down to the Kennedy Space Center in Florida. Whip hypnotized the workers into convincing them to help him and his friends go up into space. And so, our heroes built their own spaceship and off to Mars they went. After landing on Mars, they guys did research and found air-locked places like a shopping mall and a factory where Bobi's father worked. The heroes even faced danger of Martians existing on the planet. Whip fought them off.

As the guys flew home, Whip's sister, Sarah, was lost out in the streets and scientists performed an operation on her. Whip's grandfather, Ebenezer, showed up and Sarah was saved. Later, Ebenezer died and his funeral was run. Many friends and relatives were invited. The next day, Whip and his pals had their moments of a happy ending. Now the story continues…

# CHAPTER 1

## The Dream

Whip was in bed; he had a strange dream about the universe. A voice in the dream narrated: "Our world, our galaxy, and our universe meant so much to us. After an era of massive stars, space storms, and black holes, our greatest of worlds and even the largest of living spaces have come to an end." Explosions occurred. A strange figure of rabbit-like ears, a mustache and a stubby snout laughed.

"Brendor," said Whip. He opened his eyes awakening from the dream. He got out of bed in his pajamas and put a pair of slippers on. He was living in his new house with his lifetime partners. Footsteps walked up the stairs by Whip's room.

"Whip!" it was Bobi calling him. "Breakfast is ready."

"Coming!" said Whip. He walked out and followed Bobi down to the kitchen. On the table was served scrambled eggs, sausage, and bacon. As the guys ate, Whip talked about the dream he had.

"Last night, I had this weird dream about something happening to the universe," said Whip.

"It happens," said Pition.

"There's something about black holes and other things destroying it," said Whip. "I wonder if it means anything. I saw the Vip king, Brendor."

"Bad dreams just happen, Whip," said Bobi. "What would those Vips have to do with the whole universe?"

What the protagonists don't know is that the Vips will return with many new surprises. But before I can tell you *that* story, I have to tell you *this* upcoming story…

Whip's cell phone rang and he answered it.

# CHAPTER 2

## Babysitting the Givington Twins

"Hello," Whip said through his phone.

"Whip Psy, I presume," said the person calling. It was Leopold Givington, a koala who is the father of a set of twins whom Whip had babysat before.

"Mr. Givington?" Whip asked.

"Yes," said Mr. Givington. "My wife and I are about to catch a plane back to Australia tomorrow. Will you babysit my children?"

"Yes. Is it alright if I bring my friends over?"

"Are they nice people?"

"Yes, totally. We're all good guys. We'll pack some stuff and we'll be there."

"Very well." Mr. Givington hung up the phone.

"Guys!" Whip announced to his friends. "We're going back to our hometown to babysit some koala twins. Let's start packing up."

"Wow," said Bobi. "I always wanted to be with some kids." All the guys packed their suitcases and loaded their luggage in the World Bug 3000, Whip's best traveling vehicle. Whip started up the Bug's engine system. Our heroes were off to the Givingtons' house on Mumba Avenue back in Psyville.

"I never met these kids before," said Bobi. "What are they like?"

"They're the nicest kids in town," said Whip.

"I hope they know about snakes like me," said Pition.

"Perhaps they're aware of fat like mine," said Fentruck.

"Don't worry," said Whip. "William Givington is a young genius like me."

Meanwhile, at the Givingtons' house in the front yard, Mr. Givington showed his twin children a game of catch with a baseball and gloves.

"Keep your eye on the ball," he said to them as he held the ball in front of one eye. He tossed it and Will caught it.

"Got it!" he said.

"That's the second time!" said his twin sister, Agatha. Will tossed the ball back to his father. He caught it.

"Alright, Agatha, this is for you," he said. Agatha watched the ball as her father held it and he tossed it to her. As Aggie caught it, the ball slipped out of her glove.

"Butterfingers," said Will. As Aggie heard that she stuck her tongue out at her brother. She picked up the ball and tossed it back to her father. Mr. Givington held the ball in front of his face once more.

"Alright, kids!" he said. "This is the grand finale!" He tossed the ball into the air about a yard high. The twins held their gloves up. As the ball came down, Aggie opened her opened her glove as Will got in the way. The twins pushed each other around. Will caught the ball.

"Oh yeah! I win!" he shouted.

"You're such a cheater!" Aggie shouted throwing her glove at her brother. "You d—head!!" She ran in the house.

"That was a bad show," said Mr. Givington. "You two shouldn't push each other around."

"Okay, Dad," said Will.

Mr. Givington went in the house to look for Aggie.

"Agatha!" he called out. He looked everywhere in the house for her and then he found her sitting inside one of the kitchen cupboards. He opened the door and talked to her.

"You shouldn't use that language with your brother," he said.

"It's just that…" said Aggie, "…he cheats at everything. He thinks he's better than me."

"Well, Aggie," said Mr. Givington. Aggie crawled out of the cupboard. Her father continued, "He's just full of talents. Maybe you have different talents, like using your imagination and things like that."

"Does that mean I'll have better talents than Will's?" asked Aggie.

"It's just different than his. You two have a different comparison in between."

Will heard the talk as he walked by. He went into the family room to watch T.V. He sat on the couch nearest to the T.V. set. Mr. Givington walked to his work desk. He had some work to do.

Meanwhile, Whip and his pals were in Psyville and on their way to the Givingtons' house.

"We're almost there, guys," said Whip.

# CHAPTER 3

## Difficult Times

Mr. Givington told his children about the babysitter(s) coming over.

"I want you two to be on your best behavior," he said. "Whip is going to take perfect care of you while Mom and I are gone."

"I like Whip," said Aggie. "He's nice."

"Be careful," said Mr. Givington. "This house is really old and big. It's a little creaky, but it'll grow on you." He walked back to his desk to make some phone calls. In the meantime, the twins went into their bedroom upstairs to think of stuff to do. Will lifted his dumbbells up and down to exercise. Aggie sat on her bed and blew into a party blower that unrolled toward the direction of her brother.

"Want to play a game?" she asked.

"Maybe," said Will. "I'm not very moody of it."

Aggie blew in the blower. "How about *Candy Land?*"

Will sighed. "No, that's a baby's game."

"*Don't Wake Daddy?*" Aggie blew in the blower again.

"No you'll cheat."

"How about *Monopoly Jr.?*"

"No, you cheat at board games."

"But I never cheat at um...*Fireball Island.*"

"Trust me, you'll find a way."

Downstairs, Mr. Givington called Whip on the phone. Whip said he was currently on the street driving down. After that call, Mr. Givington called his wife.

Meanwhile, back upstairs in the twins' room, Aggie found a handheld fan with a container of water that can be sprayed on the person who holds it.

"Look what I found, Will," she said.

"That belongs to me, please don't mess with it," said Will.

"You don't even play with it often," said Aggie.

"So, it's still mine," said Will. "Please put it down."

"I just want to spray some water on you. I'll just turn it on and give one spray."

"Okay. Just not too much of it."

Aggie sprayed some water on her brother.

And so, downstairs at his desk, Mr. Givington talked to his wife on the phone.

"Have you bought all our supplies, honey?" he asked her.

"I'm on my way home," said Mrs. Givington.

"Okay, I'll see you then," Mr. Givington hung the phone.

Suddenly, the twins were fighting. Will ran downstairs as Aggie had broken his water fan. He carried it and shouted, "Dad!" He showed his father his water fan's blade rotor was out. "Look what Aggie did."

"I was on the phone," said Mr. Givington. "Your mom's on her way home."

Aggie appeared and said, "It was an accident."

"You're such a baby!" scolded Will.

"I'm *not* a baby!" said Aggie.

"You break all my stuff and you act like a brat and you're retarded."

"I am *not!*" Aggie shouted and grabbed a baseball from a nearby shelf and threw it toward her brother. He dodged it and the ball hit a tall room lamp and it fell over. Mr. Givington quickly ran to it and caught it from falling.

"Go sit on the couch, you two!" he said to his children harshly. The twins did what he said.

Mrs. Givington arrived home. Then Whip and his pals arrived at the house as well. Mrs. Givington went to the door and entered.

"We're just in time," said Whip.

"Hi, honey," Mrs. Givington said to her husband in the house.

"Millie," said Mr. Givington responding to his wife. "I was just talking to our kids. Are we both packed?"

"Yes, I was just getting to it," said Mrs. Givington.

"Hi, Mommy," said Aggie.

Mr. Givington went to talk to his children.

"Now I want you kids to be careful with things in this house," he said. "That lamp almost cost me another expense."

"Okay, Dad," said Aggie.

"I can keep an eye on everything," said Will.

"Mom and I are gonna fly on a plane back to Australia to meet some friends and relatives," Mr. Givington explained.

"I don't want to be alone," said Aggie.

"Well you're *not* gonna be alone," said Mr. Givington. "You'll have a babysitter here to watch you two."

Whip and his partners rang the doorbell.

"That must be him," said Mr. Givington. He went to answer the door and opened it.

"Mr. Givington," it was Whip. "We're all here."

"Come on in, boys." Mr. Givington let the guys in.

Whip approached the twins and said, "How are my two favorite critters?"

"Whip!" said Aggie.

"Hi," said Will. "Are those guys your friends?"

"Yeah, my long time good friends," said Whip. He turned to his pals and said, "Guys, meet William and Agatha Givington."

Bobi, Pition, and Fentruck introduced themselves to the twins. They shook hands (plus Pition's tail). They all settled on the furniture. Whip still stood with Mr. and Mrs. Givington.

"Should I leave you any cash?" asked Mrs. Givington.

"That's okay, I got lots of money," said Whip.

"Your mom and I are leaving, kids," Mr. Givington said to his children. "Be on your best behavior."

"Yes, Dad," said Will.

Mr. and Mrs. Givington left out the doors. And they were finally on their way to the airport. Their plan was to spend the night at a hotel and catch a plane to Australia the next day.

# CHAPTER 4

## Four Guys and a Pair of Twins

Whip, Bobi, and Pition played with a card deck at a table in the living room as Fentruck took a nap on the couch by the T.V. *Barney* was on T.V. Aggie watched some of it and Will changed the channel with the remote.

"Hey, I was watching that!" said Aggie.

"Dad said no more *Barney,*" said Will.

"He did *not!*" Aggie complained.

"We need to grow out of it." Will changed from channel to channel and came to a movie on T.V.

"Please change it back to *Barney,*" said Aggie.

"Sorry, no can do," said Will.

"Didn't *you* use to like it?"

"It doesn't matter. Times change."

"Play nice, kids," said Fentruck as he smacked his lips while sleeping. He patted on flipper on his belly.

Aggie walked around for better things to do. In the meantime, Whip, Bobi, and Pition played with cards at the living room table. Aggie went by them.

"There goes little Aggie," said Bobi.

"What's the matter?" Whip asked Aggie. "Don't you have anything to do?"

"I'm looking for something," said Aggie. "Will's watching T.V. and I want to play with him."

"Well, everybody's in a different mood," said Whip.

"You'll get used to it," said Pition.

Aggie walked into the hallway as Bobi asked, "Whip, do you have a Jack?"

"Go fish, Bobi," said Whip.

Bobi drew a card. Aggie went into a closet and found a tennis ball. She also grabbed a racket. She went back to the T.V. room where her brother still sat on the couch.

"How about if you and me play tennis?" Aggie asked him.

"No," Will answered feeling lazy.

Aggie hit the ball with the racket. The ball bounced on the floor toward Will. He caught it and tossed it back to his sister. Aggie hit the ball a second time and Will caught it again and tossed it back. The third time, Aggie hit it even harder and the racket flew out of her hand and at Will's feet.

"Ow!" he said. "You're in trouble!" He started to chase his sister as she ran around the house. Whip and his friends heard the commotion.

"Kids!" Whip called to the twins. "What's going on with you two?"

Aggie ran to find a place to hide. Will answered Whip, "We're playing hide and seek!"

"Okay, just don't run around the house like that!" said Whip.

Will looked for his sister hiding somewhere on the second floor.

"Aggie!" he said. "Don't worry, Aggie, I'm not gonna hurt you!"

Aggie hid inside a metal vent with a lever with a black rubber grip.

"Where are you, Aggie?" Will still looked for her. Then he finally found her by opening the metal door with a black handle. "There you are."

"I'm really sorry," said Aggie.

Will reached for the lever next to her.

"Don't!" shouted Aggie. "I'm not going down there."

"Well I've had enough of your behavior," said Will. He pulled the lever and the back wall opened.

"Will, no!" said Aggie. She slid down a slide that led down to the basement. *"That's not funny!"* she shouted.

"What's wrong Aggie?" Will asked. "Not so scared of basement, are you?"

Aggie reached the bottom of the slide, screaming for a few seconds.

"Whiny brats are scared of the dark below!" Will called down to her. Then he closed the vent's door. Aggie was left alone in the dark. Will went back to watch some more T.V.

# CHAPTER 5

## The Mysterious Console

Aggie found herself in a tunnel of which she crawled through to a light. She was in the basement. There appeared a laboratory of chemistry sets and science books. Aggie knew it was her brother's work lab. She found his homework desk nearby. She discovered many different things. There was equipment including a microscope, test tubes, and measuring scales and balance beams. On a metal counter nearby, there appeared something that was not there before. It looked like some sort of console. Aggie thought if it was for music or games. She was about to find out. She took the console upstairs out of the basement, carrying it in her arms. She went to the T.V. room near her brother.

"You've been very mean to me, Will," she said.

"Dad said not to sneak up on people like that," said Will.

Aggie approached him, carrying the mysterious console. "Look what I found in the basement."

Will looked at the console. "What is it?"

"I don't know. I thought *you* would know about it."

"I've never seen this thing before." Will pressed a red button that said "Power". The console unfolded a monitor screen that said, "Welcome." Then it read, "Please remain seated. It's going to be a vibrant ride."

"I think it wants us to sit down," said Will.

Aggie sat on a nearby soft chair. Suddenly, the house began to shake.

"Earthquake!" Aggie shouted.

Whip, Bobi, Pition, and Fentruck heard the commotion as well. They all gathered around.

"Just in time to finish my nap," said Fentruck.

"Something tells me we're facing a disaster," said Pition.

"An earthquake is happening!" shouted Bobi. "Save us, Whip!" He hugged Whip in a frightened mood. Things were falling and breaking.

"Let's get the twins," said Whip. The guys went to protect the twins.

"Our family pictures!" exclaimed Aggie as picture frames fell and broke. Whip and his pals protected the twins. They held onto the couches. Suddenly, the house was being lifted into the air by fiery jets. It miraculously transformed into a flying metal ship. It headed for the atmosphere.

"I think we're lifting off," said Bobi.

"Impossible," said Pition. Whip looked at the strange event occurring.

"The wood is changing into metal," he said.

"Look out the window," said Aggie. "It's getting darker the higher we go."

"Oh no!" exclaimed Will. "We're heading for outer space!"

"Are ya kidding?" said Bobi. "I've been space sick since we went to Mars."

Everyone was right to worry. The mysterious console that Aggie found was a ticket to outer space. It was also a guidance system telling them what is happening. Soon the house, now transformed into a spaceship, entered Earth's orbit.

# CHAPTER 6

## The Journey Begins

The whole gang looked around. Many things have changed since the console was activated.

"What happened?" Whip asked the twins.

"I found this weird thing in the basement," said Aggie. "Will said he didn't know anything about it."

"Maybe it's some sort of space traveling system," said Will. "That's what's going on here."

"What'll we do?" asked Aggie.

"There's a lot of things to do," said Whip. "Since we have a ship we can travel anywhere."

"Count me out," said Bobi. "I'm gonna puke." He went to a bunk bed room upstairs to lie down.

Whip sought that there was a journey lying ahead to save the galaxy from chaos. He knew about the Vips with a hideout and he knew something had to be done.

"Let me see that thing," said Whip to the twins as he sat down to look at the console. He looked at so many buttons to push that would operate different systems within the ship.

"This looks like the Starship Enterprise," said Fentruck.

Whip found a button that said "Next Task". He pressed it and the monitor screen said, "You are entering turbulence. Stand by for patrol."

"Looks like we're facing the law, guys," said Whip.

"They're not arresting me!" said Pition frightened. "I'm innocent!"

"Relax!" said Whip. "It's not bad."

# CHAPTER 7

## Space Turbulence

A space patrol arrived and entered the ship. They started to speak with the heroes.

"You have unauthorized personnel," said one officer.

"Well, I'm exceedingly sorry, sir," said Whip as he started to explain, "the thing is: we happened to have blown sky high from our planet and I'm supposed to be babysitting."

"Interesting story," said the officer. Another officer arrived.

"There is a hazardous space storm nearby," he said.

"Okay, thanks, I'll keep in touch," said Whip.

"Be careful where you fly to," said the officers. And so they left.

Our heroes were about to find out. A purple and red nebular cloud emerged in their sights.

"That must be the space storm," said Whip.

"Oh no!" cried Bobi. "We're in space turbulence!"

"No telling what's gonna happen," said Whip.

"I'm scared!" cried Aggie as she held onto her brother. The ship was being sucked into the storm.

"Could this be a black hole?!" shouted Pition.

"Hang on and enjoy the ride!" Whip said. The storm pulled the ship to an unknown place in space. The journey was only beginning.

# CHAPTER 8

## The Return of King Brendor

Meanwhile, in another place in space, there appeared a floating palace with a head with long ears, a small snout and a mustache. It was the new space palace for the Vips. In the palace's throne room sat down King Brendor. He had a teenage son named, Prince Kazam, not yet known by Whip. Whip only knew Brendor's daughter, Zelda, who was a psyvark. Kazam was a thin Vip with curved talons on his digits.

And so, a conference was settled in the room. Brendor made an announcement.

"Men," said Brendor as he announced, "I have sought the presence of our enemy specimen. Whip Psy is in outer space somewhere out there. My son will be sent to investigate."

"Yes, Father," said Prince Kazam. "My half-sister disappeared to somewhere far from Earth. I sense she will face the psyvark."

"Then go, my son," said Brendor. "Find them both!"

"Yes, I shall," said Kazam as he started to leave the palace. He flew on a ship out of the hangar bay and into space. He was on the search for his elder half-sister.

One thing is that Zelda is disguised as someone else. Well before I can tell you that part of the story, let's continue with Whip and the gang.

# CHAPTER 9

## Imogene

Whip and the others ended their journey through the space storm and ahead was a space station. They flew there and landed on a tarmac platform outside it. Everyone knew about space suits. The twins had to learn about space. Will knows a lot of science. Aggie doesn't know much so far. She had to learn that there was no air in space. Her brother helped her out. When they were all dressed, our heroes entered the station, leaving the ship. In the station were a restaurant and a research library.

"Never seen anything like this before," said Bobi.

"I always thought this happened only on T.V.," said Pition.

"I'm scared," Aggie whined.

"Just stay with me," said Will.

"Everyone, keep following me," said Whip. He had a thought in his head that occurred magically. "I sense the presence of somebody familiar."

Everybody walked into the restaurant. It looked like some perfect fashion of a diner from the 1950's. Whip met up with a girl working alone in it. The girl was a psyvark with rather long beige hair wearing glasses. As Whip looked at her, his pupils turned into hearts. He dashed toward her and started speaking, "Hi. I didn't expect to see someone of my kind here in space."

"Hi," said the girl. "Do I know you?"

"I...um...I don't think so," said Whip. "My name is Whip."

"I'm...uh...Imogene," the girl introduced herself.

"Imogene? Glad to meet you. My friends and I were just babysitting some koalas and we somehow blasted off and came by."

"Come sit with me." Imogene led Whip to a table where they sat on opposite sides to face each other and start a conversation.

"Something tells me this isn't the right place for a date," said Bobi.

Whip spoke to Imogene saying, "This place sort of reminds me of *The Jetsons*. The old Hanna-Barbera cartoon..."

"Oh yeah," said Imogene. "What else is on your mind?"

Meanwhile music played. The song "Faithfully" by Journey played.

"Aliens," said Whip.

"Are there any around here?"

"I haven't seen any," said Imogene.

"My friends and I will be around to help," said Whip.

"In the meantime, we have little koalas to protect." That made Will and Aggie giggle.

Whip remembered the time he and his friends caught the Vips and saw Brendor's daughter, Zelda, disappearing in prison.

"Is something wrong?" asked Imogene.

"Oh no, just my imagination," said Whip.

Whip and Imogene stared at each other with interest.

"They're making goo-goo eyes," said Fentruck.

"This is ridiculous," said Pition.

"It's a sexual moment," said Bobi.

"A what?" asked Aggie.

"Don't ask," said Bobi.

"It's inappropriate," said Will.

Whip and Imogene stood away from the table and touched each other, starting to make out.

Bobi and Pition panicked at the romantic moment.

"Don't tell me..." said Bobi.

The song ended as Whip and Imogene hugged and kissed each other. Moments later, Bobi went into the romantic moment.

"Okay, cut!" he said. "I think we have work to do around here."

"We'll be right with you guys," said Whip. He and Imogene stopped making out. Everyone gathered together and went to the research library.

# CHAPTER 10

## The Mystery of Omale

The gang settled in the library where it had large bookshelves with hovering boards that would allow anyone to reach up to a higher shelf. There were large computers with vocal controls that allowed anyone to speak into a microphone that commands the computers to access any subject. The largest computer in the library showed a message saying, "Today's Subject: The Mystery of Omale."

"Check this out!" said Bobi pointing to the screen. Everybody came to it. Whip used a touch pad to control the pointer. He clicked on the today's subject panel to check it out. Information came up:

"Omale is an alien gender made up of two Y chromosomes. An example is an alien race called, the Horks."

"Horks?" asked Bobi.

"Must be some kind of aliens from far away," said Whip. He looked into "horks" and read about them on the computer. "It says they are hulk-like aliens from a distant rocky planet called, Mirx. Having two Y chromosomes makes them more masculine than the male gender."

"Sounds worse than my brother," said Aggie.

"Hey!" Will shouted at his sister.

"Sorry!" said Aggie.

"They might be out exploring," said Imogene. "They, I believe, deserted their planet in search of food."

"What do they eat?" asked Will.

"Nerds, perhaps," said Bobi.

"Nerds are my favorite candy," said Aggie.

"Not those kinds of Nerds," said Bobi.

"I think he means weirdoes," said Will.

"Oh," said Aggie.

"I got a picture," said Whip as he brought up a picture of a strong, bulky, insect-headed, grapple-clawed, alien.

"EEP!" Aggie screamed.

"Shh!" said Will. "We're in public."

"I think we'd better get going," said Whip. "You're welcome to join us, Imogene."

"Sure, I'll come," said Imogene. "My diner is empty anyway."

Everybody left the library and went back to the ship. Then they took off.

# CHAPTER 11

## Invasion of the Horks

As they were leaving the station, Will and Aggie looked at the console for the next destination. It said "You will be visited by alien invaders."

"Are we in war with aliens?" asked Aggie.

"Who knows?" said Will.

"Can it be Horks?" asked Pition.

"I hope not," said Bobi.

"I can sense it with telepathy," said Whip. "It has to be Horks."

"Uh oh," said Fentruck. "We're in big trouble."

A spaceship from far away flew toward the heroes' ship. The foreign ship was shaped like the head of a horned toad.

"They don't look friendly," said Aggie.

The strange ship began to open guns and fire at the heroes' ship.

"Definitely not!" exclaimed Will. The twins hid around the ship behind chairs, under counters, etc. The Horks kept firing.

"It was your idea we wanted to meet aliens, was it?!" asked Aggie.

"There's nothing else we can do!" said Will.

Whip and the gang looked at the console. A message said, "The aliens are boarding the ship." The Hork ship approached to invade the ship. They began to make contact with each other's entrance hatches.

"Kids!" Whip called to the twins. "Better get over here! They're gonna board us!" The twins heard him and went to him. "Follow me, everyone!" Whip led the team upstairs to a safe hiding place. The Horks started to set foot in the ship. Whip and the others hid in a closet with astronaut and helmets, plus other space gear.

"Alright," Whip explained. "Everyone must keep the volume low. I'm going to see what those aliens are up to."

"Good luck, Whip," said Bobi.

"We'll keep in touch with these wrist coms," Whip showed everyone a package of communication devices that could be strapped around one's wrist. He took one out and put it on his wrist. He passed the package to Will and Aggie.

"Take one, pass 'em down," said Whip. Everybody grabbed a wrist com and strapped it on his/her wrist, except for Pition since he's a snake; he strapped his com on the base of his tail.

"Alright," said Whip, "let's test them." He pressed the button on his wrist com. "Whip to Bobi."

"I copy," said Bobi speaking through the vocal system after pressing the button on his com.

"Pition here," said Pition testing his com.

Fentruck tested *his* com, "Fentruck here."

Then Imogene, "Imogene online."

"Will," said Will.

"Aggie," said Aggie.

All the coms worked. Whip settled the new plan.

"I'm going to get to the console around those aliens," he said. "I'll let you know what happens."

"Be careful out there," said Imogene.

"Will you please?" scolded Will.

"He'll be alright," said Pition.

Whip walked out the door slowly and quietly.

"If only we had some kind of weapon," said Bobi.

Whip snuck downstairs to avoid being heard or seen by the Horks. The Horks settled in the ship's lounge. They looked at the console. Whip pressed the button on his com. He whispered, "I see the console. They're doing some kind of experiment with it."

"Whip," said Will. "Can you get to it?"

"Hold on," said Whip. "I'm coming back." He walked back upstairs.

"Is he alright?" asked Imogene.

"He's our pal," said Bobi.

Whip came back to the closet and entered it closing the door behind him. He explained, "They're all over the lounge. They must be messing around with the console. Obviously they don't know anything about it."

"Okay, we need another plan," said Pition.

"I know!" said Aggie. "Maybe one of us can go in one of the vents; only the small ones of us. There's a handle...er, a lever that opens a door to a slide. It leads down to the basement."

"Good," said Pition. "That way we can sneak past them if they're busy with other things."

"Will," Aggie turned to her brother, "do you think you can fit in that vent like I did."

"It's worth a shot," said Will.

Everybody followed the twins to the vent with the slide. They walked quietly to that place. Whip opened the two sliding doors.

"Is this the place?" he asked the twins.

"Yep," said Aggie.

"Okay, Aggie," said Will. "As I pull that lever, we'll go together. I promise I'll never let anything happen to you, 'cause you're my sister."

Aggie nodded her head. Whip bent down to the twins and asked, "Are you ready to do this?"

"Yes," said Aggie.

Will pulled the lever and made the slide appear. Then both twins slid down into the basement. Pition approached the vent and said, "They might need a bit of back up." He entered the vent and slid down to follow the twins.

The rest of the crew walked by the fence by the top of the staircase. Whip pressed his com's button and said, "Okay, kids, we're gonna make a diversion with the Horks."

"A what??" asked Aggie through her com.

"We're gonna distract them while you kids get the console," said Whip. He, Bobi, Fentruck, and Imogene were about to walk down the stairs as the Horks studied the console, pressing every button and activating every control. In the meantime, Pition and the twins walked to the doorway of the basement and walked quietly up the stairs. Upstairs, Bobi started to taunt the Horks by thumbing the sides of his head and sticking out his tongue. He made a sound "PHTFTPTPT!" Two Horks heard the sound. They went up the stairs.

"We gotta hide," said Whip. He, Bobi, Fentruck, and Imogene hid in different places. Fentruck and Bobi hid in a nearby closet. Whip and Imogene sidled to a corner wall by the rail. The Horks walked and looked for any sign of life on the upper part of the ship. Hopefully they did not see Whip or Imogene. They were cloaked with a force of invisibility.

Meanwhile, the Horks were about to carry the console to their ship. As they started carrying it, Pition and the twins made it to the lounge before the Horks' eyes. Aggie pressed her com's button and said, "We're too late."

The Horks walked on their ship and set the console on a nearby counter at the entrance. Aggie spoke in her com, "Wait, they're not leaving yet. The console is on a counter on the ship. I think I can get it." She started walking aboard the ship.

Whip spoke through his com and said, "Aggie, do not go on that ship. Just stay with your brother, we'll come and get you." Aggie still walked toward the ship.

"Aggie," said Will, "you can't..."

"Come on," said Aggie, "you gotta help me."

Will sighed and followed his sister.

"You kids are gonna get caught," said Pition. He went up to find the others as Whip oversaw the event happening. Bobi went downstairs to find something useful. Whip, Fentruck, and Imogene followed the way by the Hork ship. Whip tried contacting the twins, "Kids be careful wherever you are. Do not get the console. It's too dangerous."

"What choice do we have?" Aggie asked her brother as they hid under the counter with the console.

"Whip's right, we gotta get out of here," said Will. The twins were on the Horks' ship with cages of food animals and energy supply tanks. Will snuck off the ship while Aggie reached the console. Risking that she would be caught, she climbed up on the counter and used both hands to grab the console. Suddenly, a Hork found her yards away as she slid off the counter, carrying the console. The Hork sounded the alarm. Horks everywhere rampaged off the ship, following Aggie as she ran back on the ship with the heroes.

"Guys!" she shouted. "I have the console!" A Hork approached her and she screamed. A shoe was thrown at the Hork's head. It was Will.

"Will!" Aggie said. The Hork went back on its ship.

"I told you I'd never let anything happen to you," said Will.

"Everybody, stand back!" a voice called from the kitchen. It was Bobi waving energy-bladed knives and twirling them like a ninja. He hollered as he charged at the Horks about to slash them and stab them. The Horks ran back on their ship and escaped. The ship flew away.

"The croc is on the job, ladies and gentlemen," said Bobi.

"Wow, he's not so bad himself," said Will.

"I like his moves," said Aggie.

"Does the console still work?" Whip asked the twins. Aggie tried turning it back on. It buzzed for a moment of malfunction from the Horks. Then it was working again.

"Yes," said Aggie, "sort of."

The console brought a message saying, "Enemy reinforcements are coming in a matter of time." Its screen made fuzz and scratches.

"Something tells me it's broken because of those aliens messing with it," said Pition.

# CHAPTER 12

## The Vips' Pursuit

What the heroes did not know yet was that the Horks were in alliance with the Vips. The twins tried to figure out what was wrong with the console. Will pressed a button and the console's message screen scarped with grey fuzz.

"It won't say anything, something's wrong with it," said Will. "You killed it!" he said to his sister.

"No I didn't," said Aggie. The console suddenly got to work again.

"There it fixed itself," said Whip.

The message read, "Enemy forces about to arrive in a matter of hours."

"Are we in trouble again?" whined Aggie.

"You're such a baby," said Will.

"I'm *not* a baby!" said Aggie.

"Yeah you whine just because we're in space!" said Will.

"I'm *not a baby!*"

"YEAH?!?" The twins argued back and forth, yelling at each other. Whip tried to break up the fight.

"Kids! Stop!" he said. The twins continued yelling back and forth. Whip put his arms between their loud voices and said, "Nobody's a baby here!" He put his left hand over Will's mouth and his right hand over Aggie's. "Please! Let's all have time to share and work together. Let's all calm down."

"Okay," said Aggie as Whip took his hands off the twins' mouths.

Whip went to his friends and said, "I believe we're having more enemies coming."

"Oh no," said Bobi. "Oh boy, I can't wait to bust more moves."

Pition shivered at the moment. Imogene used telepathy to seek what was going on. It read that the Vips were coming. King Brendor and Prince Kazam were approaching a few light minutes toward the Givington house-ship. And so, the Vips entered the ship and called for the passengers. Whip, Bobi, Pition, and Fentruck came to them at the entrance.

"Brendor," said Whip.

"We meet again, famous Whip Psy," said Brendor. "I believe it's been four years since we last met at your hometown. Allow me to introduce my son, Prince Kazam." He put his hand in front of his son as he introduced him.

"I've come to look for my half-sister, Zelda," said Prince Kazam. "I sense that you have a female of your kind here, Whip."

"Her name is Imogene," said Whip. "We found her in a space diner." Kazam went up the stairs and found Imogene.

"Hello," he said.

Imogene was frightened. "What do you want from me?" she asked.

"My half-sister is in disguise somewhere around here I can feel it," Kazam explained. "You're not my half-sister, Zelda, are you?"

"What are you talking about?" said Imogene. "I don't know any Zelda."

Whip walked up a few steps and spoke to Kazam, "Considering, your highness, she's not whom you're looking for."

"Maybe you should look into her mind," said Pition to Whip.

"Look on the bright side, Prince," said Bobi to Kazam.

"I sense lies!" Kazam exclaimed.

"Come on, son, we're leaving!" Brendor called to him.

Kazam felt furious. "Since I can't find my half-sister, I'll take somebody else!" He found the two koala twins downstairs. He went down to them and grabbed them by their shirts' collars. "These two shall do for captivity." He carried them as he rejoined his father.

"Since you intrepid heroes were able to bypass my alien allies, the Horks," said Brendor, "I wish to see my daughter in my palace in a matter of hours." The Vips left the ship and flew away.

"Oh great!" said Pition. "Will and Aggie have been kidnapped!"

"'Captured' is more like it," said Bobi.

"What are we gonna do?" asked Fentruck.

# CHAPTER 13

## Koalas Captured

Whip made a confession, "There's only one thing we can do. We must follow the Vips and see what they're doing and we'll save the twins."

"Sounds risky," said Bobi.

"We'll never get to their hideout without getting caught," said Pition.

"How are we gonna save those koalas?" asked Fentruck.

"I'll go alone," said Whip. "A psyvark's gotta do what a psyvark's gotta do."

"I'll go with you," said Imogene.

"It might be dangerous," said Whip.

"I'm not sure you understand this," said Imogene. She started explaining, "The truth is…I am Princess Zelda."

"What??" said Whip.

"I am in disguise with an ego. My father does not know that."

"You disappeared in prison four years ago."

"I know. That's why I'm here."

Whip called up to his friends, "Okay, guys! We gotta fly this ship to the Vips' secret hideout."

"Oh man," said Bobi. "Talk about a *Star Trek* enterprise."

Whip went to the console and spoke into a microphone saying, "Take us to the Vips' palace."

A message on the console's screen read "The Vips' palace is far to the right and straight of here." The ship automatically moved to that direction and Whip and the others were on their way to save the koala twins.

"Hold on, kids," said Whip. "We're on our way."

And so, at the Vips' palace, Brendor and Kazam entered it as they carried Will and Aggie in a rectangular prism cage.

"What are they gonna do with us, Will?" asked Aggie.

"I don't know," said Will, "but I think they're gonna hold us hostage for a while." As the twins were brought inside the palace, they were placed on a table in the middle of the throne room. Brendor sat on his throne and interrogated with them.

"Alright," he said, "who are you kids and how did you come into space? Where did you get your ship?"

"The truth is…" said Will, "…that…the ship is not really a ship. It's our house that got transformed."

Brendor laid his head on his hand as he listened. Will continued, "I'm William Givington and this here is my twin sister, Agatha. She found some weird machine in a laboratory below our house and we turned it on and it changed our house into a spaceship."

"Interesting story," said Brendor. "Why would anything turn a house into a spaceship?"

"I don't know," said Aggie, "that's our whole problem. It must have been magic."

"Just great, Aggie," said Will. "We've been captured by strangers and we're gonna be held hostage and Mom and Dad are gonna be worried sick about us."

"I hope Whip and the others get here soon," said Aggie.

"Take them to the dungeon," Brendor ordered his minions.

"Augh!" Aggie screamed.

"Don't be afraid, Aggie," said Will. "We'll think of a way out of here." The Vips carried the twins into a dungeon below.

"I hope my old enemy comes for these koalas," said Brendor.

Meanwhile, Whip and the others arrived by the palace. Whip explained the plan, "Imogene and I are going inside the palace to save Will and Aggie. You guys stay put and guard the ship." He and Imogene went into the palace by sneaking past guards. Bobi, Pition, and Fentruck remained on the ship.

# CHAPTER 14

## Break in the Palace

As they snuck past the guards, Whip and Imogene used their hands' claws to hang on the wall of the palace. They sidled to the side in search for the dungeons. Whip believed that Will and Aggie were held prisoner somewhere. He used telepathy to know where they were.

"Follow me," he said to Imogene. He led the way to the dungeons below the palace. They started to dig a hole down to where there was no window below the first floor. They used spades and shovels.

"Are you sure you know what you're doing?" asked Imogene.

"Trust me," said Whip as he kept digging. "Will and Aggie are in the basement, I know it."

Imogene joined him in digging. This went on until they came to a brown colored lower wall below the yellow brick wall of the palace. Whip used the shovel's blade to crack a hole between two bricks. He used telekinesis to make the crack longer and break a hole in the wall. Whip and Imogene finally entered the dungeon. Meanwhile upstairs in the throne room, Brendor sought their presence.

"My daughter and the psyvark, Whip," he said. "Saving their friends, they are."

Whip followed his senses to look for Will and Aggie. Imogene followed him everywhere until Whip found the right room, where Will and Aggie set their hands on the bars of their cage.

"Whip!" they both said in surprise.

"Sh!" Whip said with one finger in front of his mouth. "We're getting you out of here." He grabbed the cage's top handle. The cage was really large so Whip carried it in his open arms. "Let's go!" he said to Imogene. They hurried out through the way they came. Suddenly, at the outer wall, a group of Vip guards appeared. Whip set the cage down and unlocked the gate.

"Okay, kids, head back to the ship," he said. "We'll take care of business here."

Will and Aggie escaped.

"The little koalas are escaping," said one of the guards.

"Let them go," said Brendor who appeared behind them all. "This is all we need right here."

Whip and Imogene surrendered with their arms up.

"So," said Brendor. "You, the one called Imogene, are a disguise, eh? Perhaps you should uncover your face with that make-up."

Imogene did what he said. She spun around in a flash of gold sparkling magic. Her hair, glasses, and casual clothing disappeared and she was back to her true form, Princess Zelda of the Vips, wearing a headdress and a white and pink dress.

"As my son said," said Brendor, "you *are* my long lost daughter, Zelda."

"You wanted me, Father," said Zelda, "now you have me."

"Imogene—er, Zelda!" said Whip.

"Go now, Whip," said Zelda. "Your friends need you." She stood by her father as Whip ran back to the ship. The guards tried to follow him.

"Let him go," said Brendor. "Our work here is done." Everybody walked back in the palace.

And so, Will and Aggie were safe aboard the ship. Whip got back on.

"Whip!" said Bobi surprised. "You made it."

"What happened to Imogene?" asked Pition.

"Let's say she's in a family reunion," said Whip.

"Huh??" said Pition and Bobi.

"She's really the Vip king's daughter, Zelda," said Whip.

"What??" said Bobi.

"That's why she's staying behind," said Whip. In the palace, Imogene/Zelda was reunited with her family. Suddenly, a call came on the TV set that had transformed into a communication system. Fentruck activated it. The screen turned on. It showed an echidna.

"Ezra Eaton?!" asked Whip.

"How are you guys?" asked the echidna.

"We're excellent," said Bobi.

"We're trying to babysit koalas and we've been driven into space," explained Whip.

"I'll have to meet up with you guys," said Ezra.

"It's good to see you again, Ez," said Whip. He turned off the screen.

# CHAPTER 15

## The Wishing Comet

Will and Aggie went to the console to activate it. A new message showed up on the screen saying "An unidentified comet is arriving. Make a wish as it passes."

"A wish??" said Aggie.

"This has gotta be the best moment of our travel!" said Will.

"I want to wish for something," said Aggie.

"I got here first so it's *my* turn to wish," said Will.

"You're a jerk!" said Aggie. "You always think you're the boss of everything."

"You're the one who got this console in the first place."

"So what? It wasn't my fault we're here."

"What do you mean it's not your fault? This is all your fault. In fact, *everything's* your fault. It's *your fault Mom and Dad left us alone!*"

"Hey!" shouted Whip.

"Bull crap!" Aggie shouted. She took off one of her shoes and threw it at her brother as he ran out of the living room. Suddenly, a beautiful white light lit up in the TV room. Will went to it and saw the comet fly by.

"I get to make my wish," he said.

"Be careful what you wish for," said Whip. "Sometimes you get something that you don't want."

"I know what I'm doing," said Will. The comet inched close to the window by the TV.

"There are both good and bad wishes," said Whip. "You gotta trust me on this."

Will closed his eyes and made his wish by whispering to himself. After the wish, the comet flew away.

"What did you wish for?" Whip asked Will.

"I can't tell you," said Will.

"Tell me," Whip said harshly.

"I have to wait until it comes true," said Will.

Whip grabbed him and exclaimed, "Tell me what you wished for!"

"Don't pinch me!" Will shrugged from Whip's grasp.

"I better check on your sister." Whip ran up the stairs to find Aggie. "Aggie!" He went into the twins' bedroom. Later, Will followed him up there and appeared to be carrying an electronic gun.

"It worked," said Will.

"Yeah, it worked," said Whip, "congratulations. We're stuck in space with one missing."

"What are you talking about?" asked Will.

"Leave him alone!" Aggie appeared under the bed nearby.

"There you are, Aggie," Whip said as he found her there, "I was worried about you." He turned to Will and asked, "What did you wish for?"

"This," Will showed him the gun in his hands.

"You wished for a toy gun," said Whip.

"It's a space blaster," explained Will, "you know every hero has one of these."

"That can be dangerous."

"You wished for a blaster?" asked Aggie. "You better not kill anyone with that."

"It's so I'm armed for battle," said Will.

"You could have wished our adventures out here were over," said Aggie. "You should've wished us out of this."

"I was under a lot of pressure, he was mad at me."

"Why were you mad at him?" Aggie asked Whip.

"Yeah, what's the big deal?" said Will. "I knew what I was doing."

"I just didn't want you to make any mistake," Whip explained, "just to make sure you two are still together. You're a family. My sister drove me crazy a lot before when she was younger. So now we gotta work together as a team. No more fighting, no more arguing."

Whip's pals entered the room.

"He's right, you know," said Pition.

Suddenly, a beep occurred on the console downstairs. Everybody went to it. The new message said "A friend has decided to visit."

"A friend??" said Bobi.

"Must be Ezra," said Whip.

# CHAPTER 16

## Ezra Eaton Returns

And so, a small ship arrived by the Givingtons' house-ship. In the small ship was an echidna, Ezra Eaton. Whip was right about him. He climbed out of his ship and entered the house-ship. Whip and his pals had come to him at the entrance.

"Ezra!" said Whip. "What a surprise."

"Good to see you guys again," said Ezra. "You looked lost in space so I thought you could use some help."

"Cool beans," said Whip. "Thanks."

"What'cha got?" asked Bobi.

"Plenty of weapons and cargo to help you guys fight aliens," said Ezra.

"I just made a wish for that," said Will. "I got a blaster."

"A wish?" Ezra asked. "Did you wish upon a star?"

"Yeah," said Will.

"Those comets are dangerous. All must be careful what they wish for."

"He did fine," said Whip. "I helped him."

"I gotta tell you a story," said Ezra. "I can see you came here with a console. I used one like that before. I had a dream about going into space. And so, I was the first echidna out here in space. But the other thing is that I had my younger sister with me in the ship I flew in. She was acting all bratty. It was about eleven years ago. We were fighting a lot back then. We had been through many adventures with aliens and other planets and stuff. When I spawned a wishing comet, I made a wish. I wished that my sister would leave me alone and go forever. After I made that wish, she began to travel to a distant world far away, and I felt terrible. We each went our separate ways. I worked on Mars, where I met Whip and his friends."

"That's right," said Bobi.

"I never got the chance to wish my sister back," said Ezra.

"It's been settled with the twins here," said Whip.

"Whip wanted to make sure we were still together," said Will.

"Oh good, perfect, says…" said Ezra, "I can't think of a rhyme for perfect."

"What's our next destination?" asked Bobi. Everybody went to the console and Will pressed the button. The new message read "Aliens are about to attack your ship. Be prepared."

"We're in trouble again," said Pition.

"Good thing Ezra got our weapons," said Bobi.

"Battle stations everyone!" Whip commanded.

Ezra gathered all the equipment for the weapon systems to fight the approaching enemies. Blasters, laser cannons and atomic shields were set all around the ship by every window. The heroes each held a firearm opening each window by them. Alien ships approached. They appeared to be more Horks. The firing began; each team fired lasers back and forth.

"I'm scared," said Aggie.

"Don't worry, Aggie," said Will. "I'll protect you." He continued firing his cannon.

# CHAPTER 17

## Another Alien Attack

The fighting went on and on. Parts of the house-ship were blown to cinders. The guys shot down much of the enemy. Many ships were blown to smithereens.

"Oh yeah!" shouted Bobi.

"Keep it up, guys!" said Whip. He shot down two more ships.

Fentruck shot down another ship and said, "I got one!"

"I think we're almost done!" said Pition. Soon there were only a few ships left. They decided to retreat and fly away.

"They're giving up!" said Will.

"For now, but I don't think it's over!" said Whip.

A beep happened on the console. Everybody went to it. The new message read "A nebula of wormholes has arrived."

"Wormholes??" asked Aggie.

"They're like holes in space you can warp through," said Will.

The ship entered the nearby nebula. There were many wormholes.

# CHAPTER 18

## Wormholes

The first wormhole took them somewhere back on Earth. They were back in their hometown of Psyville. They landed by the house of one of their high school friends, Scoobert Fletcher, a raccoon. The heroes walked off the ship and went to the front door to knock on it. Scoobert answered the door.

"Whip? Guys??" he asked. He looked at the ship in the road and went "Augh!" His eyes were wide open along with his mouth.

"I know, dude," said Whip. "We were doing some babysitting and we went into space and found a wormhole to here."

"Unbelievable," said Scoobert.

"We fought some aliens and I found a girl who turned out to be the daughter of some foreign king that I know of," Whip explained.

"Want to come inside after those adventures and cool off?"

"That's just the idea."

"We've got shelter at last," said Bobi. Everybody went into the Fletchers' house. Inside, Scoobert's kid brother, Quasimodo, was watching a movie.

*The Pagemaster,"* said Whip as he saw the TV. In that movie, pirates were studying their map and Whip quoted the following words: "It's uh…in the middle by the waterfall. No, it's east by some broccoli. Give me that. You half-wits, it's in the woods in the west by a tree." He giggled. "I love this movie."

"My brother likes watching this," said Scoobert. "He wants to be a master of books when he grows up."

"Like a librarian?"

"Sort of."

"Scoobert!" Mrs. Fletcher called from the kitchen. "Are you talking to yourself?!"

"No, Mom!" Scoobert called back. "I'm here with some friends."

"You want some bagels?" asked Mrs. Fletcher.

"You guys want some bagels?" Scoobert asked the heroes.

"We're kind of space sick," said Bobi.

"I don't think we'll eat anything for days," said Whip.

Scoobert called back to his mom, "No thanks! We're cool!"

Suddenly, another wormhole appeared. It was Job, the name-calling grey dog from high school. He ended up within the Fletchers' house.

"Job??" said Whip and the others.

Job got up and said, "Well, well, if it isn't Whip Snip and his stooges. Who's the walrus?"

"I'm Fentruck Tusker," Fentruck introduced himself.

"He's a new friend of ours from Christmas vacation four years ago," said Whip.

"Job the Globe, I presume," said Scoobert.

"Is that your nickname?" asked Quasimodo.

"Of course, Quasi...modo..." said Job, "...Ballsy...scroto." He laughed. "That'll be you, Quasimodo Ballsy-scroto."

Quasimodo laughed. Job exited through the wormhole he came through. Suddenly, a Vip's face showed up laughing wickedly.

"Brendor," said Whip. "We have to get back to ship." Everybody left the house and headed back to the ship. Suddenly, they found and ambulance with someone carrying a wheeled bed with Job.

"Oh no!" said Whip.

"Job, what happened?" said Pition.

"Something bad's..." said Job, broken from an accident that happened. "...going on. And I...Ow!...Don't know what it is."

Our heroes boarded the Givingtons' house-ship and went back into space through the wormhole they came through.

# CHAPTER 19

## An Earthly Threat

Whip used telepathy to seek what was going on. He knew the Vips were behind something big. The TV-transformed communication system's screen turned on. It showed the Vips.

"Whip Psy!" said Brendor. Whip and his pals came to the screen as Brendor continued, "You have returned for we have some unfinished business."

By his side, Prince Kazam held his half-sister who was bound and gagged.

"It's Zelda," said Whip.

"I am about to plot an attack on Earth with my alien followers," said Brendor.

"This is scary," said Aggie.

"I'm armed and dangerous!" said Will pointing his blaster at the screen.

Princess Zelda muffled with the gag in her mouth. Prince Kazam said to Whip, "You can optionally surrender to us in order to save your pretty girlfriend here." He held a knife in front of his half-sister.

"But first…" said Brendor, "there are things I want to show you." The screen showed different sections of itself with other bad guys Whip had faced before. It showed Aborabor Satvrinski reigning from prince to tsar. And there was Angus Wellington, Jr. showing anger as he sought revenge on Whip, who knew about his team cheating in the College Amusers' events. Another segment was with Martians inhabiting Mars.

"Looks like Mars has its own natives after all," said Ezra.

"We gotta do something, Whip," said Bobi.

Brendor showed his face on the screen once again and said, "Your past enemies are now working under my control." The divided screen showed up again.

"My mother's death shall be avenged," said Aborabor.

"I will win my next game for sure," said Angus.

Brendor spoke out, "Now is the time to take you back."

"Back where?" asked Whip.

Suddenly, a spiral of black and white occurred. It appeared to be a vortex. Whip and the gang got sucked into it.

# CHAPTER 20

## Déjà Vu

Our heroes entered a field near a familiar parking lot. Everything around them was black and white. The parking lot was nearby the mall. The Vips were there.

"Those Vips are up to their old tricks," said Pition.

"Talk about déjà vu," said Whip.

Suddenly, black and white versions of Whip, Bobi, and Pition appeared in a nearby bush.

"It's…" said Whip, "us!"

"There are two of you guys?" asked Aggie.

"We've been here before," said Whip. "We've been set back in time."

"There we go," said Bobi as he saw each of their past selves go inside the market.

All of a sudden, the same vortex arrived to take everyone to another time spot.

"Were you guys really brave with those Vips?" asked Fentruck.

"We sure were," said Bobi.

"We didn't know you yet, Fent," said Whip.

During the warp a picture showed Zelda in prison.

"That's Zelda," said Whip. "She disappeared from prison because of me."

The gang ended up by the Satvrinskis' palace showing the ceremonial sacrifice of Whip's sister, Sarah.

"Sarah," said Whip.

"There's me," said Fentruck as he pointed to himself in the crowd.

"I liked being a dragon," said Bobi.

The vortex took them to another place. The gang ended up in the College Amusers' triathlon.

"A shame I was blasted out of the sky when you guys won," said Fentruck.

The vortex took them to Mars. There were actual Martians inhabiting the planet, growing plants and caring for strange alien pets.

"Mars is inhabited after all," said Whip.

"There's a happy thought, says the pot," said Ezra.

The vortex returned everyone to the Givingtons' house-ship.

# CHAPTER 21

## Battle of the Vips

And so, everyone gathered together as a space fleet was led by the Vips to attack our heroes. Brendor was in command inside a mothership. He ordered the alien ships to attack. Each ship fired one shot at a time, as our heroes fired their cannons at all the ships ahead. Will had an idea. Carrying his blaster, he put on a spacesuit and called for Pition to follow him.

"Where are we going?" Pition asked Will.

"I have a plan to stop those terrible Vip guys," said Will. They exited through the ship's front door. Pition had a breathing helmet with a tank.

"This is really a bad idea," he said. He and Will entered a space pod and Will launched it and they were off to the Vips' mothership.

"I've gotta try something to stop them," said Will. The two ended up in a hatch on the bottom of the mothership. They leaped out of the pod and snuck up inside the ship. Will held his blaster up and shot any approaching Vip guards holding staffs or electric-spire spears. He and Pition fought them off as they walked through a walkway and ended up by a pit where on the other side was the rest of the walkway.

"We'll have to swing," said Will. He found a loose scrap of metal on the ceiling above the pit.

"Oh sure," said Pition. "Like I…Yah!" Will grabbed him and swung him around, throwing his head near the metal scrap. Pition bit it to hold on like a grappling hook. Will grabbed Pition's tail to hold it as he swung over the pit and landed on the next walkway.

"Childish piece of--!" Pition let go of the scrap on the ceiling as Will pulled him up with him.

"We've got to disable this place," said Will. He and Pition quietly snuck to the control room. They carefully snooped by where Brendor viewed his fleet through the front window. Nobody was in the control room. Will pulled switches off and pressed buttons to cancel the entire fleet's attack.

Meanwhile, on the Givington ship, Whip and the others saw the Vips' ships give up and retreat.

"We're winning, guys!" said Whip. "Where's Will?" He looked around and used his telepathy to find Will. He saw him on the Vip mothership disabling the fleet's control.

"Way to go, Will," he said.

Back in the mothership, Will and Pition made an attempt to rescue Zelda. They found her in a room where she sat quietly on a couch.

"Princess Zelda?" said Will.

"You shouldn't have come," said Zelda. "This place is crawling with my father's men."

Brendor and his Vips along with Prince Kazam suddenly approached the room's open door.

"So, the little brat canceled my battle strategy, eh?" said Brendor.

"Your days are outnumbered, King Brendor," said Pition.

Back on the Givington ship, Bobi said, "We've got to help the others."

"Leave it to me," said Whip. He began to perform a phantasmal dash to run super-fast with a following ghost to save Will, Pition, and Zelda from the Vips' mothership. He soared through space without a vehicle. He crashed through one of the mothership's hatches. He ran up to approach Brendor and Kazam.

"You have finally arrived," said Brendor.

"Indeed," said Kazam. "The princess is yours if you want her."

"I intend to rescue all my friends," said Whip.

Prince Kazam held a laser sword that he activated and swished it side to side. Whip had a brilliant idea. He used his mystic vision to stop time. He looked all around the ship's control panels until he found the self-destruct button; he pressed it. Time slowly started to go on and back to its original pace. The alarm rang and the radio voice spoke, "Self-destruct sequence activated. Evacuate immediately." The Vips ran off in escape pods. But Brendor and Kazam remained.

"You outsmarted us," said Brendor.

Whip went to Will, Pition, and Zelda. Whip held Will in his hands. Pition coiled around Whip's waist. Zelda held onto Whip's shoulders.

"Everybody hold on!" Whip cried out. He did his phantom dash out of the mothership and back aboard the Givingtons' house-ship.

"Whip, you're alright!" said Bobi.

Aggie ran to her brother and said, "Will! I'm so glad you're not hurt."

"Always doing my thing," said Will.

"We certainly did good," said Pition.

Zelda kissed Whip and said, "Thanks, Whip." Fentruck blushed at the sight along with Bobi and Pition.

Meanwhile, the Vips' mothership blew up with a globe of fire. The spirits of Brendor and Kazam appeared in the empty space showing anger at the heroes.

"We did it," said Ezra.

"Now all we have to worry about is getting home," said Will. Everyone went to the console and Will activated it.

# CHAPTER 22

## Another Wish

The new message read, "Unidentified comet. Make a wish as it passes."

"Another wish??" said Will. He went to the living room window and later the comet arrived. Will made a wish saying in his head, "I wish Ezra Eaton had his sister back."

As the comet flew away, a beam of light appeared with quills and a long snout. It was another echidna.

"You wished for another echidna?" asked Aggie.

"I wished that Ezra had his sister back," said Will.

Ezra went toward the echidna and said, "Mallory. I'm so glad to see you again."

"Ezra??" asked the sister echidna.

"Yes, it's me," said Ezra.

"You've grown up," said Mallory Eaton.

"So have you."

"I must have left you forever."

"It was a wish I made that was wrong. I've been working in space alone ever since."

Aggie cried at the echidna reunion. Will went to her and said, "Don't cry, Aggie."

Whip and Zelda approached the koalas to comfort Aggie.

"It's okay," said Whip. "Things like this happen a lot."

"I...know," said Aggie.

Ezra went toward Will and said, "Thanks, kids. And you guys, too. Now we have a chance to go home."

Everybody waved good-bye at the brother and sister echidnas about to leave the ship.

"Will we keep in touch sometime, Ez?" asked Bobi.

"I'll figure it out," said Ezra. And so the echidnas left in a pod on a journey back to Earth. And so, the remaining heroes went back to the console. Will pressed the button.

# CHAPTER 23
## The Black Hole

Another message appeared and read, "You've reached your journey's end. Well done."

"We're done," said Will.

"We did it?" asked Aggie.

"Good, 'cause I'm bored," said Bobi.

"We're still in the middle of nowhere," said Pition.

"Nothing's happening," said Whip. "But I'm sure it'll be something big."

"Maybe, we're home," said Will.

Suddenly, a giant black hole emerged tearing the house-ship apart.

"Black hole!" shouted Will.

"Everybody, back!" Whip commanded everyone. The black hole continued to suck pieces of the ship into its center.

"So much for home!" said Bobi.

"Great Gatsby!" said Fentruck.

"Nice knowing you all," said Zelda.

Everybody and everything drifted into space. They all were spaghettified into the black hole. They all vanished into its center and later there was utter nothingness. Whip's dream had told about the end of the universe with Brendor's face. It had all come true.

# CHAPTER 24

## Home Again

Suddenly, white light appeared. The Givingtons' house was back where it belonged. Aggie opened her eyes at the sight and ran out the door to find the trees and the neighborhood. Will sat in the family room on the couch watching T.V. Aggie put the console back downstairs in the basement. Then she went back up to her brother and said, "Will?"

"Yeah," said Will.

"We're home!" said Aggie.

"Pretty cool, huh?" said Will.

"We've had quite an adventure," said Pition.

"We *bombed* it," said Bobi.

Whip approached the twins and said, "We never speak of this, right?"

"It never happened," said both twins.

"Zelda?!" Whip called out. Zelda appeared in her alter ego.

"Call me Imogene in this form," she said.

"Okay, Imogene," said Whip, stuttering. "I was wondering. Do you like want...to get married?"

"I'd love to," said Imogene.

Whip and his friends walked out of the house. Whip told the twins, "Take care of each other, kids. Your parents will be home any time."

The twins closed the door. Whip and the crew flew away in the World Bug. A while later, Mr. and Mrs. Givington finally arrived home after their home-coming flight from Australia. The twins stood in the family room waiting for their chance to tell their parents what they had been through. The parents entered the front door. The twins went to them saying, "Mom! Dad!"

"There was this system…" said Aggie.

"And we went into space with our babysitters…" said Will.

"And we met some aliens…" said Aggie.

"And I wished for a blaster to fight against some bad guys…" said Will, "…and we won the fight against them."

"And a black hole brought us home."

"Sounds like a lot of fun," said Mr. Givington.

"Space?...Aliens?" said Mrs. Givington. "These kids have a big imagination."

The twins looked at each other and smiled, winking at one another. Imagination was the right word. Thanks to Whip and company, babysitting can possibly help kids have fun.

And so, on their ride home, Whip touched Imogene feeling romance welding inside him. He sang the song "Just the Way You Are" by Billy Joel.

And so, Imogene became Whip's fiancée.

# EPILOGUE

## What Will Happen Next?

If Whip, Bobi, Pition, and others were to go on one last adventure, where do you suppose they'll go? This might get Whip out of marrying Imogene/Zelda. A wedding will happen between the two. So go forth and enjoy the last book of this series.

Other Books by Tyler Johns

Whip

Whip 2: Whip's Christmas Adventure

Whip 3: Whip's Extreme Adventure

Whip 4: Whip Goes to Mars

The Sharp Empire

The Sharp Empire II: The Serpent Strikes Back

The Sharp Empire III: The Phantom of the Galaxy

The Sharp Empire IV: Return of the Gospel


Coming Soon:

Whip 6: The Time Bomb

Printed in the United States
By Bookmasters